DATE DUE

DE 7 '99			

YOUTH IN THE MIDDLE EAST

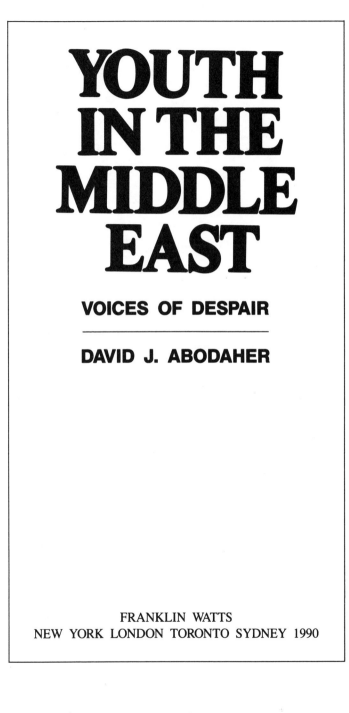

YOUTH
IN THE
MIDDLE
EAST

VOICES OF DESPAIR

DAVID J. ABODAHER

FRANKLIN WATTS
NEW YORK LONDON TORONTO SYDNEY 1990

Map by Vantage Art
Photos courtesy of: Impact Visuals: pp. 12, 92 bottom (both Neal Cassidy),
83 top, 92 top (both Judy Janda), 91 (Adam Kufeld), 105 bottom (Tordai);
New York Public Library, Picture Collection: pp. 18, 72, 96, 105 top;
AP/Wide World Photos: pp. 20, 21, 31, 34, 46, 75, 79, 81, 102; United
Nations Relief and Works Agency: pp. 32 (G. Nehmeh), 36, 49 bottom, 52
(both B. Haider), 83 bottom (Munir Nasr); Reuters/Bettmann Newsphotos:
pp. 35, 48, 49 top, 51, 86 top, 88; Woodfin Camp and Associates: pp. 56,
67 (both David Burnett); Monkmeyer Press Photo: pp. 61, 63 (Omar Bessim);
Magnum Photos: pp. 71 (R. Capa), 76, 86 bottom (both Leonard Freed);
UPI/Bettmann Newsphotos: p. 78.

Library of Congress Cataloging-in-Publication Data

Abodaher, David J.
Youth in the Middle East : voices of despair / by David J.
Abodaher.
p.   cm.
Includes bibliographical references.
Summary: Conversations with young people in the Middle East depict
the political strife there and how it has affected their lives.
ISBN 0-531-10961-5
1. Teenagers—Middle East—Juvenile literature.   2. Teenagers—
Egypt—Juvenile literature.   3. Teenagers—Israel—Juvenile
literature.   4. Teenagers—Lebanon—Juvenile literature.
5. Palestinian Arab teenagers—Juvenile literature.   6. Israel-Arab
conflicts—Juvenile literature.   7. Lebanon—History—1975– —
Juvenile literature.   [1. Middle East—Politics and government.
2. Israel-Arab conflicts.]   I. Title.   II. Title: Voices of
despair.
HQ799.M628A26   1990
305.23′5′0956—dc20   90-12254   CIP   AC

for Adam Henderson,
my much-loved and loving grandson

ACKNOWLEDGMENTS

Without many helping hands and minds, this book could not have been written. My heartfelt thanks to Ahmad Tousis, my longtime friend, and Herbert Kaufman, for the better understanding of the Arab world and Israel. My appreciation also to Abdel Gamel Shawki, public relations director for Egypt, and Abdullah Bouhabib, ambassador to the United States from Lebanon.

In no way could I possibly forget the assistance given me by Sister Emmanuel at Egypt's City of Garbage. She is perhaps the most remarkable individual I have met in my lifetime.

I cannot, of course, forget the Palestinian and Jewish families who welcomed me so warmly in Israel, and whose names were changed to offset any possible embarrassment.

I am grateful also to my friend and fellow writer Vincent Trainer for his help in double-checking research and for his encouragement.

Last, but hardly least, is the vital help given by my daughter, Lynda Henderson, in proofreading and typing this final draft.

CONTENTS

Chapter 1
In the Cross Fire
11

Chapter 2
Lebanon in Happier Days
23

Chapter 3
Lebanon Under Siege
30

Chapter 4
Lebanon's Shocking Eighties
43

Chapter 5
Egypt
55

Chapter 6
The Palestine-Israel Controversy
69

Chapter 7
The Palestinian *Intifada*
85

Chapter 8
The Young within Israel
94

Chapter 9
What Will Tomorrow Bring?
101

For Further Reading 107

Index 108

YOUTH IN THE MIDDLE EAST

1

IN THE CROSS FIRE

The voices, agonized and pleading, are those of Israeli, Palestinian, and Lebanese children and teenagers. For almost a half century, the Israeli and Palestinian young have cried out for an end to the horrors they have suffered because of political bickerings among their elders. Their Lebanese counterparts have been similarly victimized for more than a decade and a half.

Throughout those years, the young in a 12,000-square-mile area of the Middle East—stretching southward from the Syrian border at the north to a point just beyond the southeastern edge of the Mediterranean Sea—have lived under terrifying chaotic conditions. They are in constant fear of bombs and sniper bullets. They go to bed at night aware that morning might find them dead. And, indeed, thousands of young people have been killed, with many more thousands injured or orphaned, left to wander the streets and countryside, starving and homeless.

The world mourns for the innocent children and young people caught in a turbulence not of their making. It has compassion for the injured, homeless, and hungry. It decries the continuing violence. But, despite interventions by outside sources and well-meaning efforts, the killings and carnage continue.

To understand, even to a small extent, what has caused this horrendous situation, one must consider the history of the Middle East and its position on the map of the world. Equally important is knowledge of the oppressions under which the area has survived over the centuries, and its occasional domination by foreign ideologies.

Geographically, the Middle East is located at the southwestern tip of Asia and includes part of the northwestern edge of the African continent. The territory stretches from the Turkish border at the north southward to the Arabian Sea, a distance of about fifteen hundred miles (2,414 km). West to east, it ranges some seven hundred miles (1,127 km) from the Mediterranean Sea to the Persian Gulf.

In overall size, the Middle East is roughly equivalent to about one-third of the continental United States. Twenty nations exist within the area—some large, some small. Except for Lebanon and Israel, all are fundamentally Islamic in religion, whether militant Shiite or moderate Sunni Moslems. Lebanon's population is both Christian and Moslem. Israel is Jewish.

For children of the Middle East, life may appear normal at times, but all live in a state of anxiety and fear and turmoil. The young boy was shot near the eye by a rubber bullet.

Many people have the mistaken notion that Iran is part of the Middle East and that its people are Arabian. Actually Iran, once known as Persia, is considered to be the most westerly of a region designated as the Near East. Its people are not Arabic, nor do they speak the Arabic language. Their religion, however, is extremist Shiite Moslem.

Religious differences did play a minor role when the disturbances first began in the Middle East. They escalated, however, to a high point in the late 1970s. The late Ayatollah Khomeni of Iran, with his obsession to spread Islam throughout the world, brought unbelievable terror to the already vulnerable Lebanese, Palestinians, and Jews. Iran's intervention quadrupled the death, destruction, and abominable conditions that already had destroyed the fabric of good living in the area.

The Middle East is a land of ageless background and tradition, a land as old as the world itself. Many historians believe that in one section, a region between the Tigris and Euphrates rivers, the world was born. In a country once known as Mesopotamia, but now called Iraq, is the Garden of Eden, where some believe Adam and Eve were created.

In three other nearby locations nearer the Mediterranean Sea—Jerusalem, Bethlehem, and Mecca—Judaism, Christianity, and Islam, the three great religions of the world, came into being. These religions were not only born in the Middle East, but their followers have played significant roles in the history and development of the Middle East and the civilized world.

Fundamentally, all three religions are based on the existence of one God. Differences between them revolve around the birth of Jesus Christ and whether he was the Son of God, as Christians of all denominations firmly believe. While Jesus was born a Jew, and many Jews

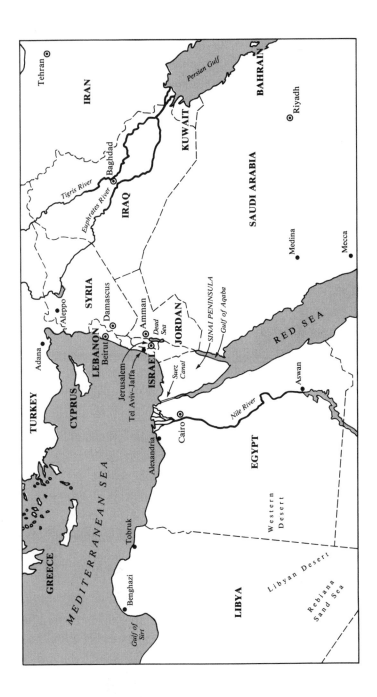

followed him to his death and beyond, the priestly hierarchy of the Temple rebuffed him. In no way, they told the people, could the son of a carpenter from Nazareth be the Redeemer the Bible promised would come to bring them peace and harmony.

In time, Jews began to accept Jesus as a great prophet, one in the mold of Abraham and Moses. The Moslems of Islam accord Jesus the same, declaring him to be a prophet like their Mohammed.

Religious differences, as the world knows too well, often lead to heated arguments, confrontations, and violence. Through countless centuries, Jews, Christians, and Moslems have been at odds with each other. Particularly in the Middle East, this has led to distrust, intolerance, bigotry, and outright violence. It should be pointed out, however, that religious differences are not the only factors that have brought about the abominable situation in the Middle East.

Another demoralizing factor has been the often changed complexion of the on-and-off control of foreign armies and governments. Only for limited periods of time have the various nations been able to govern themselves.

As long ago as 4000 B.C., the Persians and Greeks had already left their mark on the Middle East. It may have been about 1400 B.C., or a bit earlier, that the Jews, led by the prophet Moses from slavery under the pharaohs of Egypt, made their way to their "Promised Land" on the west bank of the Jordan River.

The return of the Jews in the area was the foundation for their homeland, an early Israel to be ruled by King David and his son, King Solomon. Within two centuries after the death of Solomon, the Romans moved in to rule a Jewish nation against its will. About the year A.D. 300, the Jews could no longer weather the heavy hand of the Roman

Empire; they began emigrating to countries throughout Europe, leaving the majority of the area's population Palestinians. Thus the region became known as Palestine.

In the fifteenth century, the entire Middle East was invaded by the Ottoman Empire. Through the following four hundred years, the Middle East suffered under the domination of the Ottoman Turks. Then came World War I.

The Ottoman Empire had supported Kaiser Wilhelm of Germany in the war and, when the war ended with a German defeat, the Turks were driven out. Yet the various peoples of the Middle East could not totally govern themselves. The League of Nations mandated most of the territory to England and France, and both remained in control until the 1940s.

After the second defeat of Germany in World War II, the Middle East evolved, as it is today. Lebanon was separated from Syria and made an independent nation. The other nations that now make up the Middle East achieved autonomy and self-government. Important sectors of the Middle East, however, were still denied peace and harmony.

World War II had left the Western world with a dilemma. Adolf Hitler's atrocious and bloody campaign to exterminate Jews had not only killed millions, it also left hundreds of thousands homeless and aching for a homeland of their own. This urgent and humanitarian need was considered by the United Nations General Assembly immediately after the war's end.

The issue before the UN was the creation of a nation called Israel in part of the territory then known as Palestine. The concept of a home for dispossessed Jews was not totally new. It had surfaced near the end of the nineteenth century. And, less than twenty years later, on November 2,

1917, Great Britain issued what has come to be known as the Balfour Declaration. In it, Lord Arthur James Balfour, Britain's foreign secretary, noted the following, "His Majesty's government view with favor the establishment in Palestine of a national home for the Jewish people. . . ."

The UN resolution, as it was finalized, called for a near fifty-fifty split of Palestine. The portion adjacent to the Mediterranean Sea would be the new nation of Israel. The balance, eastward to the Jordan River, would remain Palestine.

Even before Israel was proclaimed an independent nation in 1948, many thousands of Jews had already arrived in the area. And, with the Arabs seething at what they declared was unfair treatment, the seeds were sown for confrontation.

Century after century, the people of the Middle East were seldom certain as to which foreign nation governed them. They had become suspicious of their neighbors as well as of outside forces. This suspicion eventually developed into distrust and fear. Any hope for a normal existence was again shattered. Violence erupted between nations and within nations. Turmoil and turbulence became a daily diet in almost every country. The citizens of the affected countries, especially the young, suffered untold miseries.

Between 1948 and the mid-1970s, disastrous wars broke out between some of the Arab nations and Israel, with Lebanon maintaining a somewhat peaceful and happy existence. Then, in 1975, civil war broke out in Lebanon,

Orphaned children from Poland
who reached Palestine in 1944 via
Russia, Siberia, and Persia

*Armed youth of the Lebanese Socialist Party hold
their flag over a captured Lebanese army tank as
tensions rose all over that country in 1976.*

*Lebanese policemen in an armored
scout car and on foot look for snipers on
rooftops in downtown Beirut.*

and the youth of that nation, as well as their elders, were thrown into a decade and a half of unremitting assaults and killings. Neighbor turned against neighbor. Lebanon, once a peaceful and prosperous entity in the Middle East complex, had turned into a boiling pot of turmoil and turbulence.

Caught in the middle were the young.

2

LEBANON IN HAPPIER DAYS

In days long gone, Lebanese youth were the envy of most young people in the rest of the Middle East. It mattered little that Lebanon did not enjoy the wealth of oil-rich Saudi Arabia, Kuwait, Yemen, and the Emirates, wealth that helped subsidize education wherever in the world one wanted to study. Lebanese youth had something most of the others wished for.

They had freedom to live as they wished. Confining their daily lives were none of the restrictions of hardline Moslem adherence to the rules of the Koran. Boys and girls mixed, had parties, and danced.

My first visit to the Middle East included a trip to Lebanon primarily because it was the land in which my mother and father were born. That visit was in June 1971, a three-week pleasure trip with unforgettable memories.

As my flight began its descent to the airport in West Beirut, my spirits were in high gear. Below, the bright afternoon sun was reflected in the rippling waters of the Mediterranean. Beaches lining its shores were crowded with young and old. Young people could be seen lying on the golden sand or beating their way through the water. Others were throwing balls around or just frolicking.

Lebanon, with an area of barely more than four thousand square miles, is one of the smallest nations in the world. On that clear day, and with the bright sun directly behind in the west, almost all of Lebanon stretched out below. Clearly visible to the north were the spires and ruins of the cities of Byblos and Tripoli, not far from the Syrian border. Both have ancient history surrounding modern, active cities, making them certain stops for countless tourists.

Byblos is the oldest continually inhabited city in the world. Phoenician tradition explains that Byblos was founded in 7000 B.C. by the god El, who surrounded his city with an impregnable wall. Inscriptions on the early Bronze Age wall built in 2800 B.C. underscore the religious belief. It was in Byblos, not in Egypt as commonly believed, that papyrus, which made possible the production of books, was first made.

Near Byblos was the city of Tripoli, second largest in population to Beirut, Lebanon's capital. Tripoli, too, had Persian and Greek ruins worth exploring. Looking eastward, almost on a straight line from Tripoli, six great stone columns, standing perhaps as high as a five-story modern building, caught my eye. This would be Baalbek, one of the great wonders of the world. Baalbek—called Heliopolis, city of the sun god, by the Greeks—is a vast area of excavated ruins of temples and myriad other ancient structures.

Looking south through the right window of the plane, I could easily identify the even older, island city of Tyre by the causeway joining the island to the mainland. The causeway had been built in the year 323 B.C. by Alexander the Great as he tried to conquer the area. Unable to reach the island after seven months of battle, he had the causeway built and then accomplished his victory.

Tyre and its sister city of Sidon are believed to be the actual birthplace of Ancient Phoenicia—what is today known as Lebanon. Both cities were founded by nomadic Hittite and Aramaic tribes that had come west from the deserts and mountains of Arabia. They proved to be a hardy and innovative people.

Those who settled in Tyre are reputed to be the first navigators in the world. Their boats traveled as far as Gibralter and also the northern coast of Africa.

My anticipation was great as the plane touched down at Beirut airport. After checking in at the Phoenicia Hotel, overlooking the Mediterranean, it was time to see what Lebanon had to offer.

Now, eighteen years later, I ask myself what I remember most vividly of that too-short visit? Strangely, it is not any of the historic places I visited. Rather, perhaps because of the horrors to which they are now subjected, it is the euphoria of the young people of Lebanon in 1971 that is my strongest memory.

Children and teenagers revealed an unabashed openness, a freedom and lack of fear such as I had never witnessed before.

Evidence of this unusual friendliness and lack of fear of strangers came the first day. After unpacking in my room, I went down and stood on the second-level porch of the hotel. Flanking the sidewalk beneath the porch was the corniche, or boulevard, and beyond it the rippling waters of the Mediterranean. After a few moments, I became aware of two young men on the sidewalk directly below where I stood.

The pair talked for a minute or two and then, unashamedly, embraced in traditional Arab fashion and separated. One remained standing, then looked up and caught my eye. He smiled.

"You are American, yes?" he called out.

When I answered in the affirmative, he suddenly ran up the stairs and extended his hand. "Welcome to Lebanon," he said, still smiling broadly.

After a brief conversation in which I learned that his name was Nabeel and that he was just seventeen and waiting for the fall term at the American University of Beirut to begin, he suddenly exclaimed: "You must come to our home for dinner tonight. My mother and father will be most pleased to meet you."

Stunned by such unusual friendliness, my only response was a lame excuse that he would not accept. Then, no doubt noticing the chain and crucifix around my neck, he laughed.

"You are Christian," he said. "It should not matter that I am Moslem." He waited a moment, then added: "I will come to the Phoenicia at five o'clock to get you."

True to his word, young Nabeel took me to his home late that afternoon. His family—father, mother, and younger sister—greeted me with such warmth and cordiality that I immediately felt as if I had known them for years.

Over dinner and throughout a long and pleasant evening, they asked many questions about my life in America. The father, Mohammed, an officer in the Lebanese militia, was very pleased when he heard my home was in the Detroit area of Michigan. Three months earlier, he had visited Dearborn, Michigan, an area that houses the largest community of Arabic-speaking people outside the Middle East.

"I must go back for a longer visit," Mohammed said. "In one week I was able to see little more than your great

Henry Ford Museum with many old and beautiful automobiles. And I want to see also your capital, Washington, and New York, Chicago and California."

Emboldened by the family's openness and friendliness, I asked a question that was much on my mind. "Before I left home," I said, "I heard rumors of growing tension between Christians and Moslems over the fact that the president of Lebanon is always a Christian. Is that true?"

"There is always such talk," Mohammed said with a laugh. "But that is required by our constitution. Besides, both the prime minister and foreign minister are Moslems: the first a Sunni, the second a Shiite. Today there is no worry, tomorrow who knows?"

"I have had no trouble," Nabeel put in. "I play on a soccer team where there are as many Christians as Moslems. We laugh and joke together, and we are good friends."

An even more startling but somewhat similar situation occurred two days later during a taxi ride to Baalbek. Once we had covered the vast expanse of ruins, the cab driver asked if I minded stopping for a few moments at his in-laws' summer home in the nearby mountains.

Meeting the Siblani family in their mountain home was another unforgettable experience. Also Moslem, they treated me as if I were a long-lost friend. Despite all my protests, they insisted that I not only remain for dinner but also spend the night. So it was that I met their only son, Fahri, who was already scheduled to come to the United States that fall to begin university studies.

Through the course of the evening, the Siblanis asked my advice about a university Fahri might attend, one within their means. They finally decided an engineering university near my home in Michigan was the perfect choice. I was asked if I would look out for their son while he was in America and act as his guardian. It was a flattering request that I accepted.

I had not worried about any confrontation with Moslems in Lebanon. But in no way had I expected that a Moslem family would entrust me with looking out for their only son.

Everything seen during the rest of my stay emphasized the rapport that existed between Moslems and Christians at that time. In many schools, children of both religions studied together. Many close friendships were obvious. Soccer teams of young children, as well as teenagers, played, laughed, and joked together. The young in Lebanon in 1971 were a happy, joyous group, living full lives, their future as productive as they wanted to make it.

Tourism had produced a healthy economy, one almost rivaling that of oil-rich Saudi Arabia and Kuwait. It had been so for many decades, flourishing even before the nation was given independent status in 1945. The only existing tensions were in south Lebanon near Sidon and Tyre, and on the Israeli border. The Palestine Liberation Organization, fighting the Israeli occupation of what they considered their homeland, had been formed in 1964. And Israeli raids against Palestinian camps in south Lebanon at one time or another disrupted the peace and harmony.

Otherwise, Lebanon was quiet and peaceful—a far cry from the horrendous conditions that would destroy the lives of so many of Lebanon's young within five years. For the moment, at least, even the schools of south Lebanon were still open, despite bombing raids.

Educational facilities, always a Lebanese priority, were excellent. Schools had the finest teaching staffs available. The American University of Beirut, established in the 1920s by Dr. Bayard Dodge, an American professor from Harvard, offered an excellent college education to even the poorest students. Lebanese students from more affluent families enrolled at the finest universities in the United States, England, and France.

My perception of Lebanese youth as being among the most fortunate in the world persisted during that three-week visit. Even those from the poorest of families seemed to enjoy life to its fullest.

One thing seemed certain as I left Lebanon in early July of 1971. The young, whatever their faith, were well educated, cherished by their families, and cared for by their government. Under such circumstances, Lebanon would be in good hands for years to come.

Looking back now, it is inconceivable to believe that within four years, the youth of Lebanon would be under the relentless guns of an explosive anarchy. So many hundreds would die, so many thousands would be injured, and so many would see their lives and futures destroyed.

3

LEBANON UNDER SIEGE

The tragedy that befell Lebanon, with its ongoing scenario of violence, death, and destruction, erupted into the open on April 13, 1975. Tensions had been brewing below the surface for at least two years.

That fateful morning in April marked the first of three successive days in which Beirut was rocked by gunfire, rocket attacks, and bombings. Between 250 and 350 men, women, and young people lost their lives as Moslem guerrillas clashed with members of the ruling Phalangist Party. Through the rest of 1975 and into the following year, sporadic confrontations continued between the Christian Phalangists and the Moslems. Despite occasional periods of tranquility, there was no doubt that a serious civil war was under way.

Back home in America, and thousands of miles away from the scene of action, it was difficult for me to imagine the effect of this sudden upheaval on the carefree Lebanese youth I had met in 1971. To understand, it was necessary

A young man (on left) ties his family goods up
as families moved toward safer places during
the initial fighting in Lebanon in 1975.

*One of over eighty schools in Lebanon
for young Palestinian refugees.*

to look back at Lebanon's history and the subtle changes that had come about in that short period of time.

For the quarter century before Lebanon became an independent nation, and while it was part of Greater Syria, it was under the control of France, which had been given a mandate over the area by the League of Nations, forerunner to the United Nations. France is a primarily Christian nation, as was Lebanon until the 1970s. With this in mind, anticipating the day they would relinquish control, the French assisted Lebanese officials in forming the new constitution of Lebanon.

When finally approved, the constitution called for the president of Lebanon to always be a Maronite Catholic. And, bowing to the then minority Moslem population, the constitution decreed that a Moslem would always be named prime minister. This placement of the highest governmental power in the hands of Christians posed no problem as long as the makeup of the Lebanese population remained as it was. But history was about to make a radical change in that population mix.

The establishment of Israel initiated the change. Thousands of Palestinians fled to Lebanon as Palestine-Israeli troubles erupted. Other thousands emigrated to Jordan. Jordan's King Hussein worried about the thousands of Palestinians who migrated into his country. There were now as many Palestinians as Jordanites in his country, and clashes between the two became an everyday affair.

The turmoil became so aggravated, something had to be done. Hussein ordered his troops to place restrictions on the newcomers. When that failed, he gave Jordanian soldiers carte blanche to maintain order. The result was the September 1970 assault against Palestinians, forcing many to flee into Lebanon, and thousands of others to be killed in what has come to be called the Black September uprising.

*Emulating their elders, five Palestinian children
play war games in a camp in Beirut. The children
have entrenched themselves beside a shell-shattered
building and armed themselves with imitation guns.
Opposite: Scarred cinder block buildings and bullet-holed
cars provide the playground for children in a refugee
camp—when they can get out of the bomb shelter.*

The easing of the situation in Jordan intensified the problem in Lebanon. Huge Palestinian camps, three in Beirut and others in South Lebanon, helped tip the population scales in favor of the Lebanese Moslems. Inevitably, the Moslems began to demand an equal share in running the Lebanese government. When Moslem demands seemed to have been ignored, the civil war broke out in April 1975.

The on-and-off assaults of Moslems against Christians, and vice versa, continued through 1975 and into 1976. At that time, my awareness of the situation in Lebanon was kept alive by news reports and letters from Samir, the young son of another family that had befriended me in 1971. There was no mail into Lebanon, and no telephone service. My letters to Samir had to be addressed in care of a friend of his in Damascus, Syria.

There was an endless stream of on-again, off-again battles between the Moslem and Christian combatants. Almost every skirmish was followed by a short period of calm, often an open truce. When, on May 8, 1976, Elias Sarkis was elected president of Lebanon by the Lebanese Parliament, it was hoped that hostilities would end. But, it now seems, Sarkis made a critical mistake.

Sarkis had opened talks with President Hafiz Al Assad of Syria. Assad offered to send Syrian troops into Lebanon to help in ending the civil war. Many Middle East experts believed that Assad's real motivation was his desire to bring Lebanon back to its previous status as part of Greater Syria.

All that needs to be said about
the horrors of war can be seen in
the face of this small boy.

The Syrian presence was one the Palestinians in Lebanon feared, since it was known that Assad was intent on crushing the Palestine Liberation Organization (PLO) and assassinating Yasir Arafat, its head. Fierce fighting between Moslems and Christians again broke out for a six-day period beginning May 13.

On May 31, twenty thousand Syrian soldiers entered Lebanon. They did not enter Beirut, being deployed instead in the Baalbek and Bekaa Valley, an area less than thirty miles from Beirut. For a time at least, the Syrian troops seemed to be a threat, a warning to the warring Christians and Moslems to cease their confrontations or Syria would enter Beirut. But the warning did not have an immediate effect.

Clashes between the Moslems and Christians went on as before. Then, on August 12, the Lebanese Christian militia wiped out Tal Zaatar, one of the three Palestinian camps in Beirut. Every man, woman, and child in the camp was killed.

Two months later, what seemed to be a permanent cease-fire was declared, and Beirut seemed on the verge of a peaceful existence.

The probability of an end to the civil war influenced my decision to revisit Lebanon. During a phone call from young Samir (made from Damascus, Syria), I arranged to have him pick me up at the Damascus Airport, since the Beirut Airport was still closed. He did, on November 2, 1976.

As he drove me toward Beirut, seventeen-year-old Samir told me what he had hesitated to say over the telephone. His own family was now homeless. Their home had been bombed three months earlier and all five of them were temporarily living with a married sister's family.

"But don't worry," he added. "My mother has already found an apartment. We can stay there tonight even if the rest will not move in until next week."

As we drove on, he spoke at length of conditions in Beirut. He said: "Well, here it is. When you were here last time, you called Beirut heaven. Now, as you Americans would say, it's plain hell. But you will see for yourself."

That evening I did. With a curfew in effect, we had to be off the streets and in the apartment his mother had rented by seven o'clock. And, since there was no electricity, we spent the evening by candlelight. At about nine o'clock, I jumped up, shocked. The night air was suddenly echoing with the sounds of bombing and gunfire.

The outburst was no surprise to Samir. Calmly, he rose from his chair and led me to the window of the fifth-floor apartment, explaining that it faced west. Streaks of fire were darting out from right and left in concert with the loud noises of a bomb attack. This went on for some minutes, perhaps no more than two miles or so from where we stood.

"It must be near the Green Line," Samir said. The Green Line, I knew, was the point where East Beirut, the Christian sector, flanked the Moslem area of West Beirut. The blasting ended as quickly as it had started.

The next morning, we had breakfast at Samir's sister's small apartment. How was it possible, I wondered, that three adults, three teenagers, and four small children could have lived for two months in so little space—two bedrooms, a living-dining and kitchen area, and bath?

After breakfast, Samir led me through the streets of East Beirut. The number of destroyed homes and stores should not have been shocking, knowing what I already knew. But it was.

At one point, we passed a schoolyard in which a group of boys were playing soccer. The school building itself was all but gone, the victim of a shelling. At the edge of the schoolyard, a youngster of about thirteen was seated on a bench. He was facing the soccer field and, obviously, trying to hold back tears.

Recognizing the boy as a neighbor, Samir went to his side.

"What's the matter, Ali?" he asked. "Why aren't you out playing with the others?"

The boy's eyes now did fill with tears. "You ought to know," Ali sobbed. "You are a Christian. They sent me away because I am Moslem."

Walking a few steps away to give Samir time to console Ali, I could not help but wonder why the young must suffer so much at their elders' doings. Most certainly the seeds of discrimination were the fault of parents. They could not have taken into account the fact that young people cannot understand how a friend one day can be an enemy the next.

When Samir rejoined me, I asked: "If Ali is Moslem, what is his family doing here in East Beirut?"

"Many Moslems live in East Beirut," Samir explained, "and many Christians live in West Beirut. I'm sure Christian kids in West Beirut have the same problem as Ali does."

The following day Samir was busy helping his mother move into their new apartment. This gave me an opportunity to look up Nabeel and his family, the first people who had befriended me in 1971. Venturing out alone, I took a chance and went into West Beirut.

Before turning into the street on which Nabeel lived, the sound of loud talk and cries in Arabic stopped me in my tracks. A group of women surrounded and held back a young girl of perhaps fifteen. The women, it seemed, were trying to restrain the girl from running away, or worse. From their rambling talk, it was easy to discern that the teenager had a serious problem.

The girl's mother had been killed in one of the many raids. Her father was destitute and needed money, and was, therefore, forcing the girl to marry a man about five times her age. Such a marriage would bring her father a substantial amount of money.

Disbelieving what my ears were telling me, I walked on, only to be shocked again. The home in which I had been so wonderfully treated did not exist anymore. It lay now a shambles, no doubt destroyed by a bomb, a fire, or both.

Saddened, and more than a little bewildered, I walked to the shores of the Mediterranean, an area filled with happier memories. Leaning against a railing and looking down, as I had done so often in 1971, it seemed for a moment as if nothing had changed. The sea waters, far below, still lapped against rocks and cement abutments. A look to my left, however, brought me back to reality.

There was now an empty space where the classic St. Georges Hotel once stood. Not one brick of this historic structure remained. I turned and looked directly across the corniche, the boulevard which flanks the Mediterranean. The Phoenicia Hotel, at which I had stayed, was now an empty shell, its beautiful white exterior blackened by smoke.

Suddenly, some frantic cries and shouts shook me out of my thoughts. About twenty feet to my left, a teenager had leaped onto the railing and was being grabbed by three men.

"Let me alone!" the young man was screaming. "Allah is calling me."

The men soon succeeded in dragging the boy down from the railing. They led him away as he continued to struggle and scream.

That was the last distressing incident on my 1976 trip to Beirut. Two days later, Samir drove me to the Damascus airport for my flight back home.

News from Lebanon continued to be less than hopeful. On November 10, within three days of my departure,

Syrian troops, numbering 7,000, entered Beirut. If they had been sent to ease the tensions, to help end the civil war, they failed. Syria's presence merely compounded Lebanon's problems.

Over the years since 1976, Syria has remained in effective control of Lebanon. This has been so despite calls from the United Nations and other western countries for its withdrawal. By 1980, the Syrian occupation brought about an even more devastating situation for Lebanon—one that also affected many countries of the free world.

The fanatical Ayatollah Khomeni had taken over the leadership in Iran. His only friend in the Arab world was President Assad of Syria. Probably with Assad looking the other way, terrorist groups such as the Islamic Jihad and the Hisballah made their way into Lebanon through Syria. Their arrival initiated years of atrocities aimed at Lebanese, Israelis, and citizens of countries in the western world.

Hostage taking became an almost daily event in Lebanon. Residents and visitors—whether American, English, French, or German—became easy targets. Dozens of people have been taken over the years. Some have been released. Some have been killed. And some, including seven Americans, are still being held.

Lebanon was doomed and its youth were paying the price. The thirteen- and fourteen-year-olds of 1975 were now young men and women. Too many of them, having been fed a diet of discrimination and bigotry, have grown up full of distrust and malice. And the worst was yet to come.

4

LEBANON'S SHOCKING EIGHTIES

As the eighties began, the situation in Lebanon had not improved. It had actually worsened. In early 1980, a Lebanese official painted the oppressive picture in sad but colorful words:

"Our ship of state is foundering," he said. "It is being battered by the high winds of a political tornado. But we remember the words of Khalil Gibran. That does not mean it will sink."

He was referring to a quotation from *The Prophet,* a book by Lebanon's famous poet, Khalil Gibran. Published in New York in 1923, when Gibran lived in America, it is still widely available.

In his chapter on good and evil, Gibran had written: "A ship without rudder may wander aimlessly among perilous isles yet sink not to the bottom."

The Lebanese, both Moslem and Christian, are a hardy people. They do not give up, but fight with tenacity to the bitter end. With what the decade of the eighties had in store for Lebanon, they were forced to muster every ounce of fortitude.

In 1980 and 1981, the citizens of Lebanon were subjected to some of the fiercest guerrilla fighting since the civil war began. Clashes between the Christian militia and Syrian troops became more violent. In July 1981, Israeli planes struck Palestinian targets in southern Lebanon. Between July 17 and 20, air raids destroyed five bridges across two rivers south of Beirut. Air strikes against Beirut itself killed 300 people and injured 500 more.

The Lebanese economy, already in shambles because of the loss of tourists, suffered another blow when Israeli planes destroyed the terminus of the oil pipeline at Tyre. The young were principal victims of the blow to Lebanon's economy. Jobs they once held now went to fathers of families.

The following year proved to be even more harrowing. On June 6, 1982, Israel formally invaded Lebanon, determined to wipe out all Palestinian camps between its border and Beirut. There was a second objective. Having already defeated Syria in two wars in the past fifteen years, Israel was convinced it would drive the Syrian troops out of Lebanon.

Israel accomplished neither objective despite its air, land, and sea drive. It did reach the outskirts of Beirut, and on August 1 its jets bombed Beirut Palestinian camps. But more damage was done to Beirut itself than in punishing Palestinians. Ultimately, Israel pulled back, most of its troops crossing back into Israel, some remaining in south Lebanon.

Both Christians and Moslems sensed hope when, on August 23, 1982, the Lebanese Parliament elected young Bashir Gemayel as president. Bashir Gemayel was a moderate, intensely dedicated to Lebanon and concerned about its young people, who were the country's future. Unfortunately, less than a month later, on September 14, Bashir Gemayel was assassinated. It was never determined who committed this act.

To replace Bashir, his older brother, Amin Gemayel, was elected.

The new president had no chance to pursue his brother's goals. Within two days after Amin Gemayel took office, the Christian army began a day-long slaughter of Palestinians in the two remaining camps in Beirut, the Sabra and Shatila Palestine strongholds. By the end of the day, hundreds of bodies—men, women, and children— were removed from the two camps.

Just two days after becoming president, Amin Gemayel's hands seemed tied. Nothing he did, or tried to do, helped. For the next six months, Lebanon remained in torment. Then, on April 18, 1983, the American Embassy was bombed and totally destroyed in a suicidal terrorist mission. The pro-Iranian Islamic Jihad claimed responsibility for the deaths of sixty-three, including seventeen Americans.

Not long after the embassy disaster, the United States made its bid to help Lebanon. President Ronald Reagan sent a peacekeeping force of Marines into Beirut, with a complement of battleships as backup in the harbor. This inflamed the Moslems, who perceived Reagan's action merely as a means to protect the Christian government. This belief also played into the hands of the Iranian terrorists. Whoever was guilty, they wasted little time in perpetrating one of the most atrocious acts in history.

About 6:30 on the morning of October 23, 1983, a truck loaded with high explosives crashed through a series of barricades at the Marine compound in Beirut. The suicidal driver sent the truck crashing into a building in which

In the aftermath of the terrorist attack on the American embassy in Beirut in which 239 U.S. Marines were killed, soldiers search through the rubble.

American Marines were sleeping. The explosion killed 239 Marines and injured many others, two of whom later died of their wounds.

When President Reagan recalled the American forces, Lebanon was left at the mercy of the Syrians and the terrorists. Both continued to make life unbearable for Lebanon's young and old citizens.

Days and nights had become so terrifying that hundreds began to flee Beirut. Some, whose homes had been bombed, had nothing to lose and a quiet peace to be gained. Those who stubbornly remained did so to protect their property, believing that a solution might soon be found.

The young, especially the Christian youth, were in a constant state of torment. The Syrian soldiers, many of them teenagers themselves, teased and harassed Christians of both sexes. Boys were taunted with religious slurs. Girls were subjected to lewd remarks and suggestive invitations. So many such incidents took place that girls of any age feared even walking to a nearby store alone.

In one such situation, a young Syrian soldier accosted a sixteen-year-old, finally grabbing her by the shoulders when she resisted his advances. An older brother, playing catch nearby, rushed to his sister's defense, grabbing the soldier around the waist. The two struggled for a few moments. Then, as the soldier shook himself free, he drew his pistol and shot the young man.

No relief was in sight for Lebanon. The Syrians remained. The terrorists made Lebanon their base for atrocities committed against Western nations. On June 14, 1985, two terrorists believed to be members of the Islamic Jihad hijacked a TWA plane and forced the pilot to land at Beirut Airport. The plane was held for seventeen days and passengers were subjected to torture as the captors demanded safe passage out of Lebanon. A young American navy

Bulldozers clean away rubble in a Palestinian refugee camp that was bombed during clashes between the Shiite Moslem Amal militia and the Palestinians. Opposite: (top) Shiite Moslem scouts take part in a celebration in Beirut in 1985, marking the 1984 Moslem militia takeover of West Beirut from the Lebanese army. The second boy from the left carries an Iranian flag under his arm. The giant portrait on the left is of Ayatollah Khomeini; the one on the right is of Iman Mousa Sadr, founder of the Shiite Amal movement. Bottom: This classroom used to echo with the sounds of children. The school in Beirut was damaged by fighting and repaired several times.

diver was killed and his body thrown out of the plane. For the next two years, the Moslem and Christian factions continued to assault each other. The besieged Lebanese government could not stem the tide. Then, on September 23, 1988, Lebanon found itself without a leader.

President Amin Gemayel's term of office had ended. The Lebanese Parliament was unable to agree on a successor, and Lebanon was left without a president. Power in Lebanon was taken over by its small, ill-trained, and ill-equipped army. General Michel Aroun assumed leadership of the crippled Lebanese government.

Caught in the whirlpool of strife and turbulence were the youth of the beleaguered nation. Exposed daily to the gunfire and bombings, even the youngest became hardened to the violence.

The psychological effect on the lives of the Lebanese young is bound to harden elements of hatred and bigotry in the hearts and minds of future generations. The cost of war goes far beyond the number of fatalities and the damage and destruction.

Ravaged by almost fifteen years of continual fighting, Lebanon's future as a nation will certainly remain in limbo for years to come. Its young people, scarred by unforgettable, devastating memories, will carry the horrors into adulthood.

The year 1989 brought even more mind-boggling incidents that continued assaults on the young. On one occasion, a Syrian soldier misfired his submachine gun. It struck a gas tank. The ensuing explosion was horrifying in itself, but it was also followed by shooting flames that reddened the sky for miles.

Suddenly, a fifteen-year-old girl could be seen running and screaming from the flames. Her mother and father had been killed in the aftermath of a soldier's reckless shooting. She ran through the street screaming, her

*Palestinian children stand at the entrance
to a refugee camp in South Lebanon as
smoke rises from burning tires.*

dress ablaze. Fortunately, three bystanders grabbed the girl and smothered the flames.

Deadly situations such as the gas tank explosion prompted many hundreds of Lebanese citizens to flee the country. As a result, for whatever reason he had, President Assad of Syria ordered his troops to stop anyone trying to leave Lebanon.

Early on the morning of Sunday, August 6, 1989, the air over the recently peaceful port of Junni, ten miles north of Beirut, echoed and re-echoed with the nerve-racking rat-tat-tat of machine-gun fire.

A motor ferry filled with refugees fleeing to Cyprus was just pulling out of the port. An unexpected barrage from Syrian guns hit the small boat. It capsized, sending all of its occupants into the Mediterranean waters. Two young girls were drowned.

It was a heartless, senseless, and thoughtless act, explained by one soldier as "just following orders."

As 1989 neared its end, Lebanon was still in a state of upheaval and without a legitimate president. The nation was still being ruled by the military under the direction of General Michel Aroun. Aroun, it seemed, had usurped the office of president and occupied the presidential mansion.

In early November, the Lebanese Parliament met in session and finally agreed on a new president. Meeting in a remote northern town, the Parliament named René Moawad, an action resisted by General Aroun. After seventeen days in office, Moawad was assassinated by a

Children pay the highest toll in the Middle East—their future seems bleak.

remote-control bomb. General Aroun was suspected of being behind the killing. Elias Hvawi was elected to succeed Moawad.

So it is that as a new decade begins, Lebanon enters its sixteenth year of constant turmoil. Syrian troops remain deployed throughout most of the country. Terrorists continue to use Lebanon as the base of their nefarious activities against the United States and other nations of the West.

Sadly, the youth of Lebanon continue to be besieged by a debilitating situation not of their making.

5

EGYPT

Early in May 1989, it seemed worthwhile to make another visit to the Middle East. My destinations this time were Egypt and Israel.

While Egypt was at peace and now an ally of Israel—thanks to the Camp David Accord—it did have internal problems. The extremists who had assassinated President Anwar Sadat in 1981 were plaguing his successor, President Hosni Mubarak. And the fragile economy was having a sadly deteriorating effect on its young people.

The flight into Cairo International Airport was a lesson in ancient history. Below, stretching northward from desert wastes to the Mediterranean Sea, was the immortal Nile, a river that symbolizes Egypt as much as any of its many tourist attractions. It is the same river in which the baby Moses was found by the sister of Pharaoh Rameses I, and which the adult Prophet Moses turned into blood in defiance of Rameses II while freeing the Jews from his tyranny. Other evidence of Egypt's ancient times are the

Although Egypt is not at war with Israel,
it does have economic and domestic problems
that have a deleterious effect on its young.

pyramids, peaking toward the sky, and the statue of the Sphinx. Farther south are the ruins of Memphis, the capital city of the pharaohs in days long gone.

In sharp contrast are the teeming streets of Cairo, today's capital of Egypt. Its bumper-to-bumper automobiles created a scene more suggestive of New York or the Los Angeles freeways.

Next to Tokyo and Mexico City, Cairo has the largest population of any city in the world. Aware of Egypt's crippled economy, it was not surprising to notice islands of poor and neglected areas.

The Nile Hilton was my choice of hotel because it was in the very heart of downtown Cairo. Its front entrance faced the historic river and its back entrance was adjacent to Tahrir Square, around which much of Cairo's business activity revolved.

The desperation of Egypt's young became apparent the moment my taxi turned into the hotel driveway. A group of boys, no more than twelve or thirteen years old, stood on the sidewalk at the driveway entrance. As the driver swung the cab toward the entrance, one of the boys leaped in front of the car. Slamming on his brakes, the driver just missed the youngster.

It was an obvious ploy to stop the automobile, for two or three of the boys ran toward the car window at my side. Their hands outstretched, begging, all began to shout.

"American!" they cried in unison, waving their palms in my direction.

The cab driver, no doubt used to such demonstrations, muttered under his breath and then drove on toward the hotel door. The sight of the thin, emaciated youngsters and their pleading eyes left me with a feeling of guilt. There was more to come.

Settled in my hotel room, I phoned for an appointment with an Egyptian official. There was time to spare before my meeting with him later in the afternoon. I left the hotel by its rear entrance, intending to visit the fine Egyptian Museum on the left side of Tahrir Square.

Entering the square, I was surrounded by many more youngsters, all pleading for money. Most of the boys were unkempt, their clothing soiled and ragged. Each in turn expressed thanks as I gave him the equivalent of fifty American cents, and ran off. The last boy, much cleaner than the others, seemed shy. He held back until I extended my hand with double the amount given the others.

"Come," I said. Then, as he approached, I asked, "Why are none of you in school?" I had spoken in non-dialect Arabic.

"There is no school for us," he answered in an Egyptian dialect I found difficult to understand. "Of the others I do not know. My father died in the war and I must get money for my mother. It is how we live."

Impulsively, I reached back into my pocket and withdrew an Egyptian five-pound note, worth a little more than ten dollars. Holding the note toward him, I urged him to take it.

"No, no," he said, a tinge of sadness in his voice. "You are kind and have already given much money."

Looking into his now tearful eyes, I pushed the note toward him. "Take it. Any other man would have done the same, even more."

As the boy took the note, he impulsively hugged me and then kissed my hand, a gesture that represents the ultimate in thanks and respect.

He ran off, stopped for a second, and waved.

Later that afternoon, during my visit with Abdel Hamid Shawki, Director of Public Relations for President Mubarak, the multitude of young boys roaming Cairo streets was explained somewhat. Three disastrous wars against Israel within the past fifty years had destroyed

Egypt's already fragile economy. The last defeat, in 1972, took the lives of countless men. Many thousands of fatherless boys without parental discipline took to walking the streets begging, far too many of them refusing to remain in school.

From the time of its emergence as a republic in 1952, Egypt has made every effort to lose its age-old status as a nation populated by only the very rich and the very poor. It wants to erase the equivalent of a caste system that had existed for centuries.

Most of the Egyptian populace had suffered through centuries of slavery and hard labor. Before 200 B.C., they were subjugated by rulers with the title of Pharaoh, most being autocratic and dictatorial tyrants. The most familiar is the Pharaoh Rameses II, whose regime was all but destroyed when the great Prophet Moses took the Jewish slaves out of Egypt and to Palestine.

Late in the last century B.C., Egypt evolved into a monarchy ruled by kings and queens, just as autocratic and regal as the Pharaohs, but less dictatorial. Best known among the long string of monarchs are the beautiful Queen Cleopatra, who committed suicide by allowing herself to be bitten by a venomous asp, and King Farouk. Farouk is best known for his lavish and profligate life-style and for initiating the first war against Israel in 1948. An Army coup forced his abdication in 1952. In 1956 Abdel Gamel Nasser became president of Egypt.

Nasser, arrogant, hard-nosed, and a hater of Israel, tried to organize all Arab nations into a single entity dedicated to the destruction of Israel. The consortium became known as the Arab League. Egypt's name then formally changed to the United Arab Republic of Egypt, thus forming a solid tie with the other members of the League.

Nasser initiated the 1967 war against Israel, in which Egypt was defeated. He did, however, leave a lasting imprint on Egypt. The war was a heavy financial burden for the country, and, distrusting England and the United States, he received help from the Soviet Union.

Nasser realized, as none of the monarchs before him had, that Egypt's future lay in the hands of an educated population of young people. He established as many new schools as limited funds permitted and instituted needed reforms at the University of Cairo.

Nasser was also aware that Egypt could no longer remain nine-tenths desert land, that its economy would depend greatly on jobs for the poor, and on making farming possible. In trying to achieve this, he built the Aswan Dam in the area south of Cairo and began development of a means to make water available for farmlands. With his work only partly done, Nasser died of a heart attack on September 28, 1970.

Anwar Sadat, second in command to Nasser and his close ally, became president of Egypt, following Nasser's pattern for Egypt's future. Sadat, however, made one serious mistake. He began the Yom Kippur War against Israel in October 1973 and quickly saw the futility of war. His bold move in making peace with Israel has become the high point in modern Egyptian history.

Sadat contacted Menachem Begin, Israel's prime minister, by telephone and was invited to visit Jerusalem. Ignoring possible personal danger, Sadat went to Israel in early spring of 1978. Later in the year, President Jimmy Carter offered his services as mediator and also participant in further meetings.

Both Sadat and Begin came to Washington and were taken by the president to his Camp David retreat. In late September 1978, what has come to be known as the Camp David Accord became a reality. Israel and Egypt would be at peace and establish diplomatic relations. Angered by

While many people think of sophisticated cities like Cairo when they think of Egypt, the country actually consists of many poor rural areas like this one.

Egypt's treaty with Israel, the rest of the Arab world turned against Sadat.

The western nations, however, hailed Sadat for his initiative and commended Menachem Begin. The Nobel Peace Prize for 1978 was awarded jointly to Sadat and Begin. Within three years, however, Anwar Sadat was dead, the victim of an assassination by Egyptian extremists.

As my interview with Egypt's Public Relations Director neared its end, Shawki noted that Hosni Mubarak, Sadat's successor, had been in office about eight years. During that time, he had worked hard to stabilize Egypt's fragile economy. And, Abdel Shawki added, much was being done to get roving youngsters off the streets and into school. Caring people outside the government were also helping. It would be beneficial, he told me, to visit what Egyptians called the "City of Garbage."

City of Garbage? This town with the foul and ugly name was already in my plans for the next day. It had been the subject of a segment on the television program "60 Minutes" about a year earlier. It was an example of what one dedicated person could do to save unfortunate children.

When I arrived at the City of Garbage about noon the next day, the horrible stench all but turned me away. The more than 25,000 people of the town were the garbage collectors for the city of Cairo, a few miles distant. Everywhere young children, teens, and adults were pulling carts heaped with refuse of all sorts.

One youngster, perhaps thirteen or fourteen, came toward me, smiling broadly and laughing loudly as he tugged at his loaded and smelly cart.

"Why are you so happy doing such work?" I asked the boy.

*Various Egyptian leaders have known that an
important way to maintain peace and a healthy
economy is through education. These youngsters are
in a classroom in a new village in upper Egypt.*

"Sister Emmanuel says one can bear even the worst kind of work if one is happy," he answered.

When I asked if he did this all day, he gave me another warm smile and said, "No. When I have finished with this load, I will go to school at Sister Emmanuel's."

Arriving at Sister Emmanuel's compound, I was amazed to find a seventy-nine-year-old woman with the spirit and energy of a healthy person in her forties. She greeted me warmly, her handshake strong and firm.

"How brave you are to come here!" she exclaimed.

"I could not leave Egypt," I said, "without meeting the only saint I would ever know in my lifetime."

Sister Emmanuel, a French nun, had been a professor at the University of Cairo. At the age of sixty-two, she was arbitrarily ordered by the church to retire.

"It was not something I wished to do," she said, her tone a bit sad, "so I prayed and asked God to direct me." She looked into my eyes for a moment, then went on. "I asked God to send me to the most wretched place in the world so I might help people. He sent me here. That was seventeen years ago and I am still here."

When Sister Emmanuel arrived in 1971, she found a colony of Egyptian outcasts—people who, for a hundred years, had picked up trash discarded by the citizens of Cairo. They lived on the food they could salvage, on the metals and articles that could be used or sold.

For months after her arrival, Sister Emmanuel was looked down upon and despised by the people she had come to help. But she never gave up. She held fast to her conviction that she could gain their trust if she lived her life as they did. She did, and the people of the City of Garbage finally accepted her.

"I came here," she told me, "to help put meaning into their lives. No outsider had ever come before me. I came to share their misery and despair, be despised as they were. In this way, I felt certain that in time they would realize that they are no less human beings and children of God than others."

It was no easy task for the former proud professor. When she came, she lived in shacks as they did, ate as they did, suffered with them. Today the adults of the City of Garbage love her and come to her for advice.

Sister Emmanuel accomplished the nearly impossible by showing herself to be no better than the people. She began her life there in a tiny shack, a far cry from the living quarters she enjoyed in Cairo. Garbage was all around her tiny home. Little by little, as the people looked to her for help, she changed their way of thinking and their lives. She helped them build modest homes to replace their own ramshackle huts. She taught them how to grow vegetables for their food. She did everything possible to give them a sense of dignity and belief in themselves.

The townspeople reciprocated. The tiny shack in which Sister Emmanuel first lived was replaced by a bright metal house built for her by volunteers. And everything else I could see could be described only as a miracle.

Sister Emmanuel built a compost factory to dispose of unusable trash. She had schools built. A kindergarten has more than 300 children. A fine high school, her great pride, includes some 800 students. Every young person will leave school, she says, with a future other than collecting garbage. The high school cost a million dollars to build and staff.

How did she do all this? Sister Emmanuel is an expert fund raiser. Much of the money came from Catholic charities, even though at least one-third of the children are neither Catholic nor Christian but Moslem. The Egyptian government has helped as much as it could and is planning similar projects in other areas, hoping to move the beggars off the street and into the classroom.

A sudden burst of shouts in Egyptian turned my eyes toward the entrance to the high school. A swarm of students had burst through the doors, some of the boys carrying soccer balls, which they tossed in the air. Girls followed quietly, turning into an area away from the male students.

One of the errantly thrown balls came rolling toward me. The boy who came for it stopped to greet Sister Emmanuel as I handed him the ball. He then smiled in my direction.

"Salaam," he said cheerily, "you are American?"

I nodded. "What is your name?" I asked.

"Samir Madi," he answered. "Someday I will go to America. When I finish high school, I will join my brother in Cleveland, Ohio. I will help him fix automobiles."

"You must be doing well here in school."

"One must do better than good," he said, looking toward Sister Emmanuel. "Sister is very tough. Why, she will not let us in school if we are not clean."

With that, he turned and ran off, tossing the soccer ball to a classmate. Sister Emmanuel laughed.

"Discipline is necessary with these children," she told me. "They have little or none at home. So I am hard, perhaps too hard sometimes. But it must be so. Boys and girls must perform well, and so must the teachers and other staff."

Sister Emmanuel paused and looked out toward the play area. "You see," she finally added, "it is much better that they are here playing and learning than walking through Cairo begging. Here they have a chance to make something of their lives."

As in every country, the future
of Egypt lies with its young.

As I prepared to leave, I thanked Sister Emmanuel for her kindness.

"Earlier," Sister told me, "you called me a saint. In your book, please don't say Sister Emmanuel is a saint. She is only a poor human being trying to help other human beings to be as good and productive as they can be."

It had been a most inspiring and rewarding visit. Egypt was indeed lucky to have a Sister Emmanuel. And the young people whose lives she changed were the most fortunate of all. How wonderful it would be if other governments would fund schools such as those in Egypt's City of Garbage.

The next morning it was time to leave for Israel.

6

THE PALESTINE-ISRAEL
CONTROVERSY

The youth in another area of the Middle East have been subjected to lives of apprehension and fear little different than those of their brethren in Lebanon. This is the region immediately south of the Lebanese border, sandwiched between the west bank of the Jordan River and the Mediterranean Sea.

It is that part of the Middle East once known as the homeland of the Jews. Later, and for centuries after, it was known as Palestine. For the past forty years or more, that territory has been the center of hostility between two cultures.

As in Lebanon, religious differences have played only a miniscule role in the lengthy disagreement that has resulted in the same horrifying devastation that has plagued the people to the north. The core of this bilateral controversy lies, rather, in who legitimately belongs in the territory.

As long ago as the sixth century B.C., the area was little more than a no-man's land, occupied at intervals by various nomadic tribes. When the great prophet Moses freed the Jewish people from the tyranny of the Egyptian pharaohs, he led them out of Egypt to what the Jews called their "Promised Land." When Moses, because of ill health, could not complete the lengthy journey, his aide, Joshua, brought the Jews to the banks of the Jordan. There they settled, to establish the first homeland of the Jews, one that became the first Kingdom of Israel. Jerusalem, where King Solomon built the first Temple, became the heart of Judaism.

Historically, the Jews were the first to occupy the territory on a permanent basis. They remained there until the Roman invasion made their lives uncomfortable. About A.D. 500 they began emigrating to countries throughout Europe. The Palestinians moved in about that time and ruled the land even though many Jews still remained. What had been a Jewish state was now a nation called Palestine. It would remain so until after World War II.

Jews in Europe began returning to what was once their homeland around the turn of the twentieth century. They came in small numbers initially, but the exodus began to reach the thousands during World War II. Adolf Hitler's massacre of millions of Jews in Germany and Poland precipitated a rush from Europe to Palestine.

After the war ended, compassionate members of the United Nations began a move to solve the need of the Jewish people to have a home of their own. In 1947 the UN decreed that the territory known as Palestine would be divided. The area along the West Bank of the Jordan would remain Palestinian. A little more than half of the region, that along the Mediterranean, would become the new nation of Israel. Instead of bringing peace, the UN action brought down the wrath of the entire Arab world.

*A woman and her young son—part of east
European immigrants arriving in a reception
camp near Haifa, Israel, in 1948.*

The result was an unending scenario of death and destruction throughout the following forty and more years. Terrorism became the rule of the day, beginning in November 1947, on the day after the UN resolution was passed. Palestinians attacked Jewish settlements in the holy city of Jerusalem. Less than five months later, in early 1948, Menachem Begin led a group of his Irgun followers in a retaliatory measure.

(The Irgun was the counterpart of the Palestinian terrorist factions. Begin, its leader, would later become prime minister of Israel.)

On a fateful morning, Begin took the Irgun to a small village named Dar Yassin, near Jerusalem. More than 250 Palestinian men, women, and children were massacred. Sixty-four were killed in one building.

The horror of Dar Yassin, and the prospect of more to come, impelled thousands of Palestinians to flee the area. Many crossed the Jordan River into Jordan. Others fled across the border into Lebanon. At least a million remained.

The new democracy of Israel was in little danger. Quickly, with the help of the United States, it developed a

Top: Princess Mary Avenue in Jerusalem is turned into "Barbed Wire Alley" during the last days of the British Mandatory Government. The wire was laid by the British to prevent Jews and Arabs from coming into contact with each other. Bottom: Part of a British poster written in three languages describing twenty-nine men —some members of the Irgun group—who escaped in a mass jailbreak in 1948.

well-trained, well-armed defense. Its assaults on Palestinians were carefully planned. The Palestinians, on the other hand, conducted raids impulsively.

Four days after the Dar Yassin disaster, the Palestinians, aided by other Arabs, got even in an equally bloody coup. They ambushed a Jewish medical convoy and brutally murdered seventy-seven doctors and nurses. This atrocity took place just four days before Israel was to be officially designated an independent and sovereign state.

Meanwhile, seven other Arab nations decided to join the Palestinians in an all-out effort to destroy Israel. Their armies stormed into the Palestine area to initiate a seven-month-long demolition of Israel. Their effort was in vain. Before the seventh month was completed, all Arab forces were back in their own countries. Israeli strength had prevailed.

The next fifteen or so years were dotted with helter-skelter, hit-and-miss attacks by the Arabs and retaliations by the Israelis. In 1964 the Arabs regrouped. Arab leaders gathered in Jerusalem to form the PLO, the Palestine Liberation Organization, and elected Yasir Arafat as chairman. Now more care was taken in planning, with more devastating acts of terrorism on the agenda.

The Palestinians and their PLO, as well as the other Arab nations, refused to accept what should have been obvious. There was no way in which the PLO, even with Arab nations' help, could do as they claimed they would do. They could never destroy Israel and "push it into the sea"—not when the United States and other western nations were committed to Israel's defense. Assaults by the Arabs continued. Israel was just as relentless in fighting back.

In 1967 both Syria and Egypt warred against Israel. Both were defeated, with Syria losing territory, the Golan Heights.

*Jewish fire fighters try to put out a fire on
buses set aflame by Arab shellings.*

One of the most horrible and senseless acts of terrorism ever perpetrated came about in 1972. It was carefully orchestrated by the PLO and occurred, not in Israel, but in Germany. On September 13, a group of Palestinian terrorists entered the residential compound of the Olympic Games then taking place in Munich. When the siege finally ended, eleven Israeli athletes, five Palestinian terrorists, and one police officer were dead.

This senseless, arbitrary assault on the Olympic athletes was one the PLO and Palestinians would forever regret. The civilized world as a whole abhorred the act and turned against them. Even Arab nations condemned the action. Most badly damaged was Yasir Arafat, chairman of the PLO. Any slight perception of him as a useful diplomat for the Palestinian cause was erased.

Israel, in shock over the murder of its athletes, was in for more trouble in 1972. Egyptian President Anwar Sadat began an attack on Israeli territory. Egypt's armed forces crossed the Suez Canal into the Sinai Peninsula, land it had lost to Israel in the 1967 war.

Hoping to catch Israel off guard on Yom Kippur, the most solemn Jewish holy day, Egypt took over part of the Sinai. Israel, however, quickly recovered and Egypt again lost.

The defeat of Egypt did have a bright side. It was a prelude to some measure of peace in the Middle East.

Arab refugee families, who left
Israel and the occupied territory
after the Six-Day War in 1967, coming
back from Jordanian refugee camps
to Israel. They are being
helped by Israeli soldiers.

*Flags at half-mast at the 1972 Olympics
during a memorial service for the Israeli athletes
slain by Palestinian terrorists*

*The Yom Kippur War in 1973 caught Israel
by surprise. Although Israel defeated Egypt,
the loss of Israeli lives was great.*

Anwar Sadat had obviously recognized the futility of trying to destroy Israel. As a brave and wise man, he decided to do something positive. In October 1977, he made a brave and risky move that would surely bring down the wrath of other Arab nations.

With his nation's future at stake, Sadat phoned Menachem Begin, the Israeli Prime Minister. Discussions between him and Begin resulted in an invitation to visit Israel. Sadat arrived in Jerusalem on November 19 and remained there until November 21. Talks and an agreement in principle with Begin were followed by Sadat's addressing the Israeli Knesset, the nation's legislative body.

The free world outside the Middle East applauded Sadat for risking his own life with a visit to the enemy camp in the interest of peace. President Jimmy Carter of the United States offered his services as mediator in the peace process. He invited both Begin and Sadat to Washington. They accepted Carter's invitation to a summit at Camp David in the Maryland hills. There, in the Fall of 1978, the now-famous Camp David Accord was reached, a signed treaty of peace between Egypt and Israel.

The terms of the accord included a hope that other Arab nations would follow Sadat's example. It was a vain expectation. Every Arab nation turned on Sadat and isolated him and Egypt from the Arab League. Sadat stood his ground, and diplomatic relations between Israel and Egypt were initiated.

Meanwhile, Palestinians and Jews continued to attack each other. Israel launched bomb attacks against the PLO and Shiite Moslem camps in southern Lebanon, bombing the historic cities of Tyre and Sidon. The Palestinians, backed by the Shiite groups, assaulted Israeli cities across the Lebanese border.

Thinking of Sadat's courage in finding a pathway to peace might well have influenced Yasir Arafat. In the early

*Yasir Arafat (right), chairman of the
Palestine Liberation Organization*

1980s, Arafat became more conciliatory in his attitude toward Israel. While he did not immediately recognize Israel's right to exist, or denounce terrorism, he softened his rhetoric.

Arafat's backing down incensed the more militant members of the PLO. A splinter group broke away from the Arafat-led faction and proceeded to muddy the long-awaited peace action.

Arafat, determined to erase his image as a terrorist, continued to ease the tone of his declarations. In late 1987, with the moderate and open-minded Israeli Prime Minister Shimon Peres, Arafat openly declared Israel's right to exist and renounced terrorism.

Hope for progress was soon shattered, though. Within months after the extremist, hard-line Yitzhak Shamir succeeded Peres, Palestinian dreams faded. Shamir sent hundreds of soldiers into the West Bank and Gaza Strip. Severe restrictions were placed on movement in and out of the territories. Israeli soldiers searched all Palestinian homes for arms of any kind. All Palestinian schools were shut down.

This decision by Prime Minister Shamir backfired. Palestinian parents were inflamed. Not only did it deprive their young people of their education, it left them, on the West Bank and in the Gaza Strip, free to roam the streets.

Where once happy Palestinian children attended school . . . now stand empty classrooms as a result of the Intifada, *the Palestinian uprising, and Israelis' closing down schools.*

Even within Israel itself, outcries against Shamir's intransigent policy became commonplace. Also, the outside world began to question Shamir's judgment. The United States, Israel's closest ally, protested. Shamir arbitrarily dismissed the American protests, declaring that no foreign government had a right to interfere in Israel's problems.

More Israeli soldiers were sent into both the West Bank and Gaza Strip to continue to intimidate the rebelling Palestinians, further escalating an abominable situation in which young Palestinians played a heart-rending role.

7

THE PALESTINIAN *INTIFADA*

The scene would shock even the most insensitive onlooker—it was unbelievable and horrifying. The time is late in 1987. The locale is the West Bank of the Jordan River. Hundreds of Palestinians faced a long line of Israeli soldiers. Men, women, children, and teenagers screamed at the men in uniform.

"Go back where you came from!" one Palestinian teen shouted.

"Give us back our homes!" another cried out.

A chorus of young and old pleaded: "Let us live in peace!"

The extended line of Israeli military charged forward, pushing the Palestinians back. Suddenly a barrage of stones, bottles, and other debris showered the soldiers. They raised their guns, loaded with dummy bullets, and fired a salvo of shots into the protesting crowd. Many, mostly children and teenagers, fell to the ground—some badly injured, a few killed.

This confrontation was the beginning of the *intifada*, an Arabic word that roughly means a brushing off of, or a resistance to, an unwelcome situation. Filmed by American and European news cameras, the incident sent a shock wave throughout the world.

A similar protest had occurred almost simultaneously in the Gaza Strip. It, too, was photographed widely and seen on television in many parts of the world. Anti-Israeli repercussions were felt by Prime Minister Shamir. Though shamed by the image of Israel as a murderer of children, Shamir became more unyielding. He sent more troops into both areas.

Meanwhile, Yasir Arafat continued to be more conciliatory toward Israel. Despite more extreme factions inside the PLO, he repeated again and again that Israel had a right to exist. What he wanted now was a resolution of the rights of Palestinians to have a home of their own in the portion of the territory given them by the United Nations decree.

Prime Minister Shamir would not accept Yasir Arafat as a spokesman for the Palestinians. To Shamir, Arafat was still a terrorist, and Shamir would not agree that people can change. He persisted in denouncing Arafat even when reminded that Menachem Begin, a former prime minister of Israel, had been a terrorist in his youth and had changed enough to finally sign the peace accord with Egypt.

Top: A Palestinian youth hurls a stone, which he fires from a large sling toward Israeli soldiers outside Jerusalem. Bottom: A typical scene in an Arab town on the West Bank. Teenagers and young children form the ranks of the Intifada, *the Palestinian uprising in the occupied territories.*

Seven children of one household in
a refugee camp in the Gaza Strip
pose on the only bed in their three-room
shelter. The family has nineteen members.

Not even the often-made suggestions by the American, British, and French governments that he soften his stand moved Shamir. He continued to insist that it was an Israeli problem and that he, as prime minister, was doing what was best for his people.

Inside Israel itself, there was a growing clamor that Shamir take a more open-minded view. The unrest of so many citizens over Shamir's policy had obviously carried over to members of the Knesset, the Israeli parliament. When the Knesset met on November 1, 1988, to elect a new prime minister, Shamir failed in his bid for re-election.

To remain in office, Shamir had to find a coalition he could live with. The previous coalition of religious hard-liners had disintegrated. He turned back to Shimon Peres's Labor Party. After some discussions with Peres, Shamir garnered enough votes to keep his post as prime minister.

Perhaps as a result of his agreement with Peres, Prime Minister Shamir finally made one concession. While he still would not recognize Yasir Arafat as the leader of the Palestinians, he offered an opportunity for Palestinians to hold free elections in the West Bank and Gaza Strip areas. Implicit in this softening of his stance was the hope that someone other than Arafat would emerge as the spokesman for Palestine.

Shamir's proposal was not greeted with enthusiasm by either the Palestinians or the Arab nations. As of the end of 1989, the elections had not taken place.

The Palestinians had organized their *intifada* as a means of alerting the outside world to their predicament. They did not immediately put it into effect after Shamir's re-election. They had waited weeks, hoping that the way in which Shamir retained his office would soften his hard stance. When nothing happened, they began their protest.

Though the *intifada* was an embarrassment, the prime minister of Israel remained unshaken. He issued another order. No foreign correspondents or television cameras were to be allowed inside the West Bank or Gaza Strip. No outsider would then know of any further throwing of rocks and bottles or indiscriminate shooting of protesters by his Israeli troops.

Shamir continued to impose tight restrictions on all Palestinians on the West Bank and in Gaza. Movement was confined to the immediate vicinity of homes. Leaders who spoke out against the tight controls were arrested and jailed without trial. Some fled. Some were exiled. Israeli troops made unannounced visits to Palestinian homes to search for arms, seizing any that were found.

The meeting of minds between Prime Minister Shamir and Shimon Peres that helped Shamir keep his post had given every indication that some statement favorable to the Palestinians might be forthcoming. This did not happen. Instead, there were more clashes with Israeli soldiers and, less than two weeks after Shamir's re-election, Yasir Arafat made a bold move. He proclaimed that the new nation of Palestine did exist and that Jerusalem was its capital. In light of the United Nations decree, he was justified in stating that the nation of Palestine existed. However, naming Jerusalem as its capital city was reckless and meaningless.

For one thing, the Israeli Knesset had officially named Jerusalem as the capital of Israel, and the government had been moved there. In addition, many people throughout the free world firmly believed that Jerusalem should be neither Palestinian nor Israeli. It was the Holy City, cherished by Christians, Moslems, and Jews alike. It should be named a free and independent area, open to all who practiced any one of the three religions.

*The real victims of war. Two youngsters stand
in the destroyed doorway of their home.*

Children have always played war games. However, this form of play takes on frightening meaning when it reflects a real war going on, as evidenced by these children playing "Intifada." Below: Palestinian youths march near Hebron on the West Bank to celebrate the first anniversary of the Intifada.

During the seven-month period before and after the beginning of the *intifada,* more than a hundred Palestinians were killed, most of them children and teens. More than a thousand had been injured, some seriously.

The outside world became more shocked at the continued carnage. Even the American government under President Ronald Reagan made harsh criticism of the Israeli prime minister's seeming lack of compassion. Shamir's only answer to reaction from outside his own country was to re-open some of the schools he had ordered closed months before. Not all closed schools were included. His edict applied only to a hundred elementary schools, thus taking the youngest children off the streets.

The *intifada* did not end. Deaths and injuries to young people continued almost daily. Some nations saw the urgent need to try anything in order to stop the deadly confrontations between Palestinians and Israelis.

King Hussein of Jordan, who had, in June 1988, removed himself as a mediator in the controversy, decided in November 1989 to again become involved. He announced that he was ready to do whatever he could to bring about some measure of peace.

The Soviet Union then also entered the picture. Its foreign minister arranged a meeting between Yasir Arafat and the Israeli foreign minister. It was held in Cairo, with Egyptian President Hosni Mubarak taking part in the discussions. Nothing tangible resulted from the meeting, as Israel continued to refuse acceptance of Arafat as spokesman for the Palestinians. Israel's single concession was to suggest open elections on the West Bank and Gaza Strip as one way to begin serious talks.

8

THE YOUNG WITHIN ISRAEL

There is little doubt that the young people of Israel have been victimized by the horrors of the *intifada* as much as the Palestinian youth have. This is true of Arab as well as Jewish children and teenagers living in Israel.

To see for myself how Israeli youths have reacted to the abominable situation, I made a trip to Israel in mid-May 1989.

As my plane prepared to land at Tel Aviv Airport, the sight below was as interesting, geographically and historically, as the view over Cairo. The waters of the Mediterranean tossed and shimmered under the brilliant May sky. Tel Aviv looked peaceful, belying the torment in which Israel found itself.

Some distance further east, two larger-than-lake-sized pools of water sparkled. One had to be the fabled Sea of Galilee, the other the Dead Sea. There was no mistaking the long, narrow ribbon of water that flowed north to south.

That was the river Jordan. The land beyond the far side of the river would be the nation of Jordan.

My eyes turned away from the Jordan River and searched for the city of Jerusalem. With its Wailing Wall, the last remaining portion of the ancient Temple of the Jews, it was easily discernable. A surge of action some distance beyond Jerusalem then caught my attention. As the plane began its descent, it was easy to identify what was going on. Clearly visible was a crowd of adults and young people with arms raised, throwing rocks. Also visible was the row of soldiers holding submachine guns. The scene was identical to many seen on television back home. The *intifada* was on in full swing.

After checking into my hotel, it was necessary to quickly plan my all-too-brief visit of three days. I immediately telephoned two families—one Israeli, the other Arab—whose names I had been given. Both families greeted me warmly. The Israelis—Julian and Sarah Kohn —invited me to dinner that same evening. Their eighteen-year-old-son, Joel, would pick me up at the hotel at five o'clock.

With about four hours of waiting ahead of me, I decided to take a stroll through Tel Aviv. Near a street corner not far from the hotel I paused to look around at the beautiful city built from the ground up about forty years earlier.

On the opposite side of the street, a group of boys, the oldest perhaps fifteen, stood talking animatedly. Suddenly, three of the youngsters darted out into the path of oncoming traffic. Two threw themselves at moving automobiles. The third missed the car he aimed for and fell at the curb not far from where I stood.

Brakes screeched and the traffic halted. Men ran out into the street to pick up the two boys who had been injured

by the impact with the moving cars. The third boy just brushed the back end of a moving vehicle and fell at the curb. A policeman rushed to grab the young man.

"You fool!" the officer shouted. "Is what you are doing worth killing yourself for?"

"Nobody can say we are not as brave as Palestinians!" the boy exclaimed as the officer led him away.

Shocked, unnerved, and hardly understanding what had happened, I returned to the hotel. A clearer picture of what I witnessed emerged that evening at the Kohn home.

"Our boys have heard too much about the rock-throwing on the West Bank," Julian Kohn told me. "It is their way of showing their own bravery."

"It's terrible," Sarah Kohn put in. "Already two boys have been killed and at least six badly injured."

"Nobody can say we are cowards," sixteen-year-old Aram exclaimed.

"Shut up, Aram," Joel told his younger brother.

"It's all right for you to say," Aram countered. "In less than a year you will be in the army doing good."

"That's different," Sarah told her youngest son. She turned to me and added: "You see, when an Israeli young man [also woman] reaches nineteen, he must spend three years in the army." She shook her head sadly. "The younger ones have become too impatient. What they are doing is no good."

"Yes, it is," Aram exclaimed. "We show we are just as brave as Palestinians. Joel will show how macho he is when he is in the army and carries a gun!"

Israeli young people as well as Palestinian youth have been victims of the conflict in the region.

"Aram, use your head!" Joel said. "Do you think I'm going to enjoy shooting at boys and girls? They may be Palestinians, but they are also human beings."

"Listen to your brother, Aram," Mrs. Kohn said. She turned to me. "That is the real tragedy," she added. "Our soldiers are as much victims as the children they are ordered to control. The psychological effect on their young minds will haunt them the rest of their lives."

"We all suffer," Julian Kohn said. "It affects us all. When we Jews meet an Arab on the street, we stare at each other with a hollow, meaningless glare. Perhaps it is because we both feel a sense of guilt. But let us change the subject. What are your plans? Is there anything special you'd like to see?"

Explaining that I had little time, but that I had great hope of at least seeing Jerusalem, Julian Kohn offered to take me there the next morning. He refused to take no for an answer.

On the trip to Jerusalem the next day, I was still shaken by the incredible way in which young Israelis risked their lives in order to show themselves to be tough.

"You must understand," Sarah Kohn told me as we rode along, "that our young are proud. They have been hurt by the way in which American journalists have given the world a picture of Palestinian young people as willing to take chances. They feel a need to show themselves as equally brave."

"Our young have little to do," Julian added. "They have too much time on their hands."

He went on to point out that the Israeli economy was in a state of shambles. There were few jobs for the young and even pay for adults was low. As a result, young people could not afford even such diversions as a cassette recorder to fill spare moments.

"It is our inflation rate," Julian said. "For as long as I

can remember, it has hovered around the 100 percent mark."

Once we arrived in Jerusalem, both Mr. and Mrs. Kohn did not speak any more about the difficulties suffered by young Israelis. Instead, they pointed out the historic wonders of the Holy City. They showed me the ancient churches and synagogues.

On the way back toward Tel Aviv, the Kohns dropped me off in Beit Hanina, a small village not far from Jerusalem, at the home of the second family in Israel I was to visit. It was mid-afternoon when we arrived. The Ayalla family was in their yard, adjacent to the house. Mr. and Mrs. Ayalla were seated at a table under a tall palm tree. In the farthest part of the yard were two young boys. As I started toward the table, I realized that the name Beit Hanina means "house of contentment." How much peace and contentment, I wondered, could a Palestinian family enjoy in Israel, despite the name of their village?

Ishmael and Lisa Ayalla greeted me in the typical warm Arabic tradition. We sat for a few moments exchanging pleasantries. Then Ishmael called to his two sons.

"Come and say hello to our visitor from America!" he called out.

Both boys came and said their hellos shyly. One seemed a little more reserved than the other.

"You are from America?" the older boy said. "How I wish I could go to school in your country." With that, both returned to play in the rear part of the yard.

Lisa Ayalla excused herself and went inside. Ishmael and I continued talking about their situation as Palestinians living in Israel.

"We have no trouble," Ishmael said, "as long as we remain in Beit Hanina. There are many Palestinian families here and we mix only with each other."

He went on to explain that his family were also victims of the high inflation rate in Israel. They, too, had a difficult time making ends meet.

"It is the children who suffer most," he said. "They have little to do but go to school. Mohammed, my oldest son, wishes to go to school in America as some of his cousins have done. But we do not have the money."

Mrs. Ayalla returned with demitasse cups of rich Turkish coffee. She then seated herself and joined in the conversation.

"We have to be very careful," she said. "We have to act as if we know nothing about the *intifada,* and we must worry about the young ones at Nablus, the city where the rock-throwing goes on. It is not far from here, but we do not dare go near Nablus."

After a fine dinner of Arabic foods, the Ayalla family called me a cab. They had no car.

"We can't afford one," Ishmael apologized.

Returning to my hotel in Tel Aviv, I prepared to leave Israel the next morning.

9

WHAT WILL TOMORROW BRING?

As the year 1989 faded into history, there was only one answer to the question of what tomorrow would bring to these countries and their people: only time would tell.

As the decade of the nineties began, there was little or no improvement in the lives of the young in Lebanon, in Egypt, in Israel, and on the West Bank or in the Gaza Strip. Children and teens were still under the gun.

In Lebanon

There has been little change in the chaotic situation in Lebanon. Children and teenagers continue to pay the dire emotional price. More have been killed, more injured, more made homeless and orphaned.

The Syrian troops remain in control. The terrorist organizations funded by Iran continue their horrendous atrocities.

For a brief moment in December 1989, there was a glimmer of hope. The Lebanese Parliament finally agreed

on a new president. However, General Michel Aroun, chief of the Lebanese militia, refused to accept the parliamentary decision and refused to leave the presidential palace.

Unfortunately, the new president was assassinated within a week of his election. At the moment of this writing, there seems little chance that peace in Lebanon is possible in the immediate future.

In Egypt
The youth of Egypt are the least vulnerable and are far more able to withstand the pressures of their nation's weakened economy.

While many still suffer and continue to roam the streets begging, many more have returned to school to pursue an education that will form the basis for a productive future.

The country itself is relatively at peace. There are, nonetheless, extremist groups that keep Egypt's government on edge. The same hardliners who killed former President Anwar Sadat have declared that one day they will succeed in destroying Hosni Mubarak, Egypt's current president.

In Israel
Here, too, the problem is unchanged. Prime Minister Itshak Shamir remains in power, stubbornly refusing to accept Yasir Arafat as spokesman for the Palestinians.

A three-year-old Lebanese Christian girl wearing full army dress holding an automated weapon—an ominous note for the future.

Soldiers continue to control the West Bank of the Jordan and the Gaza Strip. Confrontations have not ended. Nor is there any indication that there will soon be an end to the hostilities.

For the youth of Israel there is, at least, one bright ray of light. No longer are young boys throwing themselves at automobiles in a show of bravado.

On the Palestinian Front

The weekend of December 8, 1989, marked the two-year anniversary of the horrendous *Intifada*. It has not weakened in its intensity. Young boys and girls continue to throw rocks and debris at Israeli soldiers in an ongoing reminder to the world of their plight.

More young lives are sacrificed to rubber bullets. Countless more are injured, many seriously. The young Palestinians consider being sent to a hospital as a badge of their courage. They look upon being shot as a sign of their undying commitment to a cause.

But the cause is no nearer a solution than ever. This despite the fact that the United Nations is seriously considering the declaration of the West Bank and Gaza Strip as the new nation called Palestine.

It is, perhaps, a vain hope. Even though the United States has openly agreed that the Palestinians should have a homeland of their own, it has threatened to withdraw all funding for the United Nations if that body makes such a declaration.

Both young Israelis and Palestinians face a future of uncertainty and instability.

This is, obviously, a contradictory position on the part of the American government under President George Bush. Without the establishment of Palestine as an independent state, there can be no peace. And yet the American creed is a determination to help bring peace and democracy to the entire world.

FOR FURTHER READING

Abdallah, Maureen. *Middle East.* Englewood Cliffs, NJ: Silver Burdett, 1986.

Carroll, Raymond. *The Palestine Question.* New York: Franklin Watts, 1983.

Friedman, Thomas L. *From Beirut to Jerusalem.* New York: Farrar Strauss & Giroux, 1989.

Kublin, Hyman. *The Middle East: Regional Study.* Boston: Houghton Mifflin, 1973.

Rabinovich, Abraham. *Jerusalem on Earth: People, Passions, and Politics of the Holy City.* New York: Free Press, 1988.

Shapiro, William. *Lebanon.* New York: Franklin Watts, 1984.

Stetoff, Rebecca. *West Bank-Gaza Strip.* New York: Chelsea House, 1988.

Ventura, Piero. *Journey to Egypt.* New York: Viking Kestrel, 1986.

Viorist, Milton. *Sands of Sorrow: Israel's Journey from Independence to Uncertainty.* New York: Harper & Row, 1987.

INDEX

Alexander the Great, 25
American Embassy, 45
Arab League, 59, 80
Arafat, Yasir, 74
   and Assad, 38
   and Israel, 80–82, 93
   and Palestine, 87, 90
   and Shamir, 103
   and terrorism, 77–78
Aroun, Michel, 50, 53–54, 103
Assad, Hafiz Al, 37–38, 53
Aswan Dam, 60
Ayalla family, 99–100

Baalbek, 24, 38
Balfour Declaration, 19
"Barbed Wire Alley," 72
Begin, Menachem, 60, 62, 73, 80

Beirut, Lebanon, 21, 34–35
   in 1971, 25–29
   in 1976, 39–42
   air strikes in, 44
   Palestinians attacked in, 45
Beit Hanina, Israel, 99
Bekaa Valley, Lebanon, 38
Black September uprising, 33
Bush, George, 106
Byblos, Lebanon, 24

Cairo, Egypt, 57–58
Camp David Accord, 55, 60, 62, 80
Carter, Jimmy, 60, 80
Christians, 14
   in Lebanese government, 33

Christians (*continued*)
    and Moslems, 27–28,
      30, 37
    and Palestinians, 45
    and Syrians, 44
City of Garbage, 62–68
Civil war in Lebanon, 19,
    22, 30–42
Cleopatra (Queen), 59

Dar Yassin village, 73
David (King), 16

Egypt, 55–68, 103
    and Israel, 74–77, 79
Emmanuel (Sister), 64–68
England, 17, 19

Farouk (King), 59
France, 17, 33

Gaza Strip, 82–84, 87–90,
    93, 104
Gemayel, Amin, 45, 50
Gemayel, Bashir, 44–45
Germany, 17, 77–78
Gibran, Khalil, 43
Golan Heights, 74
Greeks in Middle East, 16
Green Line in Lebanon, 39

Hijacking, plane, 47, 50
Hisballah terrorists, 42
Hitler, Adolf, 17, 70
Hittite tribes, 25
Hostage taking, 42

Hussein (King), 33, 37, 93
Hvawi, Elias, 54

Immigration to Israel, 71
Intifada, 85–93, 104
    Israeli youth, 94–98
Iran, 14
Irgun group, 72–73
Islam, 14, 16, 42
Israel, 11, 103–104
    formation of, 17, 19,
      33
    invasion of Lebanon
      by, 44
    and Palestine, 44,
      69–84
    and PLO, 80
    war with Arab
      nations, 59–60,
      74–77, 79
    and West Bank, 82–
      84, 87–90, 93, 104
    youth within, 94–100

Jerusalem, 70, 72–73, 90
Jesus, 14, 16
Jihad terrorists, 42, 45,
    47, 50
Jordan, 33, 37, 73
Joshua, 70
Judaism and Jewish people
    and Balfour
      Declaration, 19
    and Jerusalem, 70
    and Jesus, 14, 16
Junni port, Lebanon, 53

Khomeni (Ayatollah), 14,
42
Kohn family, 95, 97–99

League of Nations, 17, 33
Lebanon, 11, 33, 37
  bombing of PLO in,
    80
  civil war in, 19, 22,
    30–42
  current situation in,
    101–103
  in 1971, 23–29
  in 1980s, 43–54
Lebanon Social Party, 20

Marines, attack on, 45–47
Mesopotamia, 14
Moawad, Rene, 53–54
Moses, 16, 55, 70
Moslems
  and Christians, 27–
    28, 30, 37
  emigration of, 37
  in Lebanese
    government, 33
Mubarak, Hosni, 55, 62,
  93, 103
Munich, Germany, 77–78

Nablus, Israel, 100
Nasser, Abdel Gamel, 59–
  60
Nobel Peace Prize, 62

Olympic Games, 77–78

Ottoman Empire, 17

Palestine and Palestinians,
  11, 17, 70, 73
  in Beirut, 45
  current situation for,
    104–106
  emigration of, 32–33,
    73
  and *intifada*, 85–93
  and Israel, 44, 69–84
  rights sought for, 87
  and UN, 19, 104, 106
  and West Bank, 82–
    84, 87–90, 93, 104
Palestine Liberation
  Organization (PLO)
  and Assad, 38
  formation of, 28, 74
  and Israel, 80
  splintering of, 82
  and terrorism, 77–78
Peacekeeping forces, 45–
  47
Peres, Shimon, 82, 89–90
Persians, 16
Phalangists, 30
Phoenicia, 25
Poland, 18
Promised Land, 70

Rameses (Pharaoh), 55, 59
Reagan, Ronald, 45, 47, 93
Religious factors in Middle
  East, 14, 27–30, 33,
  37, 40–42, 45, 69

Romans, 16–17

Sabra camp in Beirut, 45
Sadat, Anwar, 55
    attack on Israel by,
        77, 79–80
    and Camp David
        Accord, 60, 62, 80
Sadr, Iman Mousa, 49
Sarkis, Elias, 37
Shamir, Yitzhak, 82–84,
    87, 89–90, 103
Shatila camp in Beirut, 45
Shawki, Abdel Hamid, 58,
    62
Shiite Moslems, 14, 48–
    49, 80
Siblani family, 27–28
Sidon, Lebanon, 25, 28,
    80
Sinai Peninsula, 77, 79
Solomon (King), 16, 70
Soviet Union, 60, 93
Syria and Syrians
    and Christians, 44
    formation of, 17
    and Israel, 44, 74
    in Lebanon, 37–38,
        47, 101
    refugees attacked by,
        53

Tal Zaatar camp, 38
Tel Aviv, Israel, 95, 97
Terrorism
    in Lebanon, 42

at Olympic Games,
    77–78
renounced by Arafat,
    82
TWA plane hijacking,
    47, 50
after UN resolution,
    73
and US marines, 45–
    47
Tripoli, Lebanon, 24
Turks, 17
TWA plane hijacking, 47,
    50
Tyre, Lebanon, 24–25, 28
    bombings at, 44, 80

United Nations
    and Israel, 19, 70, 73
    and Palestine, 17,
        104, 106
United States
    and Israel, 73–74,
        84, 93
    and Lebanon, 45–47
    and Palestine, 104,
        106

West Bank, 82–84, 87–
    90, 93, 104
Wilhelm (Kaiser), 17
World War I, 17
World War II, 17, 70

Yom Kippur War, 60, 77,
    79

ABOUT THE AUTHOR

David Abodaher began writing in his teens, his first published efforts being novelette mysteries for what then were called pulp magazines. While still pursuing his university studies, he also created radio dramas that included such network features as "Famous Jury Trials" and "Smoke Dreams." After service in the United States Signal Corps during World War II, Mr. Abodaher returned to Michigan and began a career writing advertising for automobile manufacturers. It was during this period that he began writing books for young people. This is his thirteenth book for that audience.

Mr. Abodaher is a history buff with hobbies ranging from sports and reading to extensive travel. The father of one daughter, Mr. Abodaher has a grandson and lives in Southfield, Michigan, a suburb of Detroit.